Let's Go!

Car Rides

By Pamela Walker

Children's Press
A Division of Grolier Publishing
New York / London / Hong Kong / Sydney
Danbury, Connecticut

Photo Credits: Cover, pp. 5, 7, 11, 13, 15, 17, 19, 21 by Thaddeus Harden; p. 9 by Angela Booth
Contributing Editor: Mark Beyer
Book Design: MaryJane Wojciechowski

Visit Children's Press on the Internet at:
http://publishing.grolier.com

Cataloging-in-Publication Data

Walker, Pamela, 1958-
    Car rides / by Pamela Walker
    p. cm.—(Let's go!)
    Includes bibliographical references and index.
    Summary: Simple text and photographs describe riding
in a car, including fastening seat belts, stopping for red lights,
and driving at night.
    ISBN 0-516-23100-6 (lib. bdg.)—ISBN 0-516-23025-5 (pbk.)
    1. Transportation, Automotive—Juvenile literature
[1. Transportation 2. Automobiles]   I. Title II. Series
    2000
388.3—dc21

Contents

I like to ride in the **car**.

I sit in the back seat and look out the window.

5

My mom keeps both hands on the **steering wheel**.

We always wear our seat belts.

7

There are other cars on the road with us.

I see a blue car and a white car.

9

When the **light** turns red, we stop.

The other cars stop, too.

ONLY

RAMSEY, N.J.
New Jersey
WP·373B
Ramsey AUTO GROUP

LEGACY

OUTBACK
AWD

11

When the light turns green, we go again.

Now people who want to cross the street must stop.

13

Sometimes I like to ride with the window open.

The wind blows back my hair.

15

Sometimes we make other stops.

My mom stops to buy food.

I carry the **shopping bag**.

Sometimes we drive at night.

It's dark inside the car.

We can see the lights of the car in front of us.

19

I get very tired from long car rides.

Sometimes I'm sleeping when we get home.

New Words

car (**kar**) something with four wheels and a motor that takes people places

light (**lyt**) a light at a street corner that tells car drivers to stop or to go

shopping bag (**shop**-ing **bag**) a bag that holds things from a store

steering wheel (**steer**-ing **weel**) a wheel inside a car used to make the car turn

To Find Out More

Books
Big Book of Cars
by Trevor Lord
DK Publishing

Cars! Cars! Cars!
by Grace MacCarone and David A. Carter
Scholastic

Web Sites
Chevron Cars
www.chevroncars.com
This site has games and fun car facts.

Sloan Car Museum
www.ipl.org/exhibit/sloan
This site shows cars from the Alfred P. Sloan Museum. Here you can learn about the history of car making.

Index

About the Author

Pamela Walker lives in Brooklyn, New York. She takes a train to work every day, but enjoys all forms of transportation.

Reading Consultants

Kris Flynn, Coordinator, Small School District Literacy, The San Diego County Office of Education

Shelly Forys, Certified Reading Recovery Specialist, W.J. Sahnow Elementary School, Waterloo, IL

Peggy McNamara, Professor, Bank Street College of Education, Reading and Literacy Program